Especially for _____

From _____

ACKNOWLEDGMENTS

The editor and the publisher have made every effort to trace the ownership of all copyrighted material and to secure permission from copyright holders of such material. In the event of any question arising as to the use of any material the publisher and editor, while expressing regret for inadvertent error, will be pleased to make the necessary corrections in future printings. Thanks are due to the following authors, publishers, publications and agents for permission to use the material indicated.

DODD, MEAD & COMPANY, for an excerpt from *Letters To A Teenage Son* by Henry Gregor Felsen. Copyright © 1961, 1962 by Henry Gregor Felsen, Dodd, Mead & Company.

GIBSON GREETING CARDS, INC., for "What Is A Baby" and "That First Baby Will Prove 'It's The Little Things That Count' " by Helen Farries. Reprinted by permission of Gibson Greeting Cards, Inc., Cincinnati, Ohio.

VANCE, ELEANOR GRAHAM, for an excerpt from *For These Moments* by Eleanor Graham Vance. Copyright © 1939 by Eleanor Graham Vance.

WALLIS, DR. CHARLES L., for "God's Way" by E.T. Sullivan from *The Treasure Chest*. Copyright © 1965 by Dr. Charles L. Wallis.

Illustrations from

THE ORIGINAL PETER RABBIT BOOKS®
by Beatrix Potter
Copyright © 1902, 1904, 1907, 1909, 1910, 1911, 1918, 1932, 1935, 1937, 1938, 1939, 1946,
F. Warne & Co., London and New York.

Copyright © MCMLXXXI by
The C. R. Gibson Company
Norwalk, Connecticut
ISBN: 0-8378-1932-6

a little book about baby

Beatrix Potter Collection™

The C. R. Gibson Company, Norwalk, Connecticut

WHAT IS A BABY?

It's a soft little bundle
Of sweetness and charms
To be cherished and cuddled
And held in your arms . . .
It's a sweet little treasure
So priceless in worth
There's nothing so precious
On all of this earth . . .
It's a wee bit of sunshine
To make your days bright,
It's a star in your heaven
That shines through the night . . .
It's a gift and a blessing
That comes from above,
And it's your living symbol
Of God's perfect love!

Helen Farries

When the first baby laughed for the first time, the laugh broke into a thousand pieces and they all went skipping about, and that was the beginning of fairies.

James Barrie

Name _____

Born on _____

at _____ o'clock _____ M.

Place _____

Weight _____ Height _____

Color of Eyes _____ Color of Hair _____

Doctor _____

Nurse (s) _____

THINKING OF BABY

Baby awake is a mischievous elf
Who can keep you busy
In spite of yourself!
A rollicking, frolicking,
     gurgling sprite
Who may sleep half the day . . .
(And cry half the night!)

But yet when you're humming
     a last lullaby,
And the sandman has come
And closed each little eye . . .
Gone is the elf, and you find
     out instead,
You've just tucked a tired
     little angel in bed.

Author Unknown

PHOTO OF MOTHER AND BABY

. . . there is one picture so beautiful that no painter has ever been able perfectly to reproduce it, and that is the picture of the mother holding in her arms her babe.

William Jennings Bryan

ONLY A BABY SMALL

Only a baby small
   Dropped from the skies,
Only a laughing face,
   Two sunny eyes;
Only two cherry lips,
   One chubby nose;
Only two little hands,
   Ten little toes.

Only a tender flower
   Sent us to rear;
Only a life to love
   While we are here;
Only a baby small,
   Never at rest;
Small, but how dear to us,
   God knoweth best.

Matthias Barr

The night you were born, I ceased being my father's boy and became my son's father. That night I began a new life.

Henry Gregor Felsen

PROUD PARENTS

_____

_____

and GRANDPARENTS

_____ _____

_____ _____